BIG BOOK OF BRICK TRUCKS

15 of Your Favorite Vehicles!

Amanda Brack

Sky Pony Press
New York

Car Carrier

When cars need to go long distances, such as to be sold at a car dealership, car carriers can drive them there!

Cement Mixer

This heavy truck pours cement. Cement is used to make roads and sidewalks!

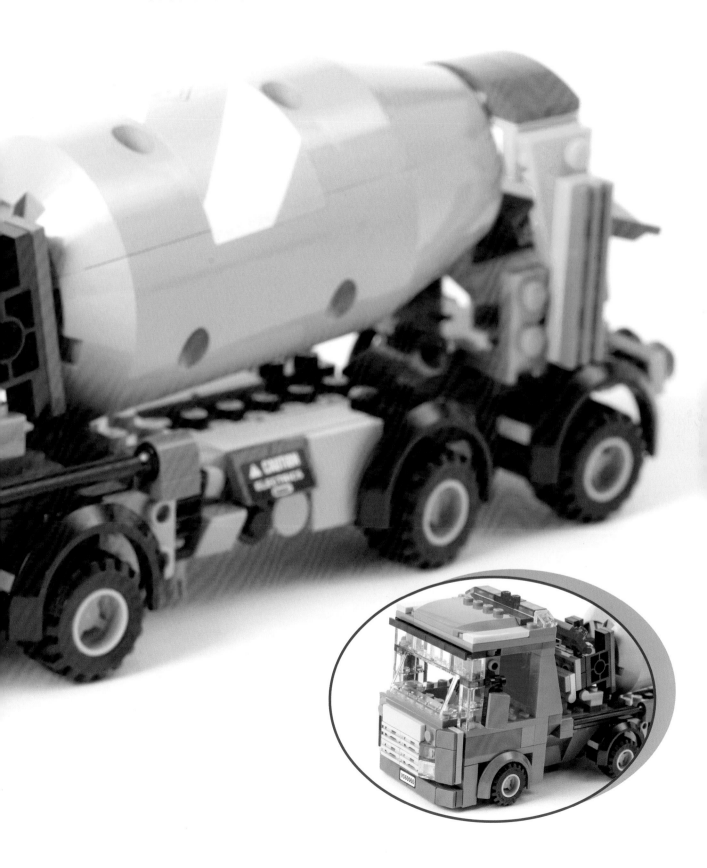

Dump Truck

This big truck can hold lots of things! The back door opens so whatever it is carrying can be dumped out.

Fire Engine

When big things are burning, the fire engine will save the day! Firefighters use big hoses on the truck to spray water and put the fire out.

Garbage Truck

What a stinky truck! The garbage truck picks up our trash and carries it away to the dump.

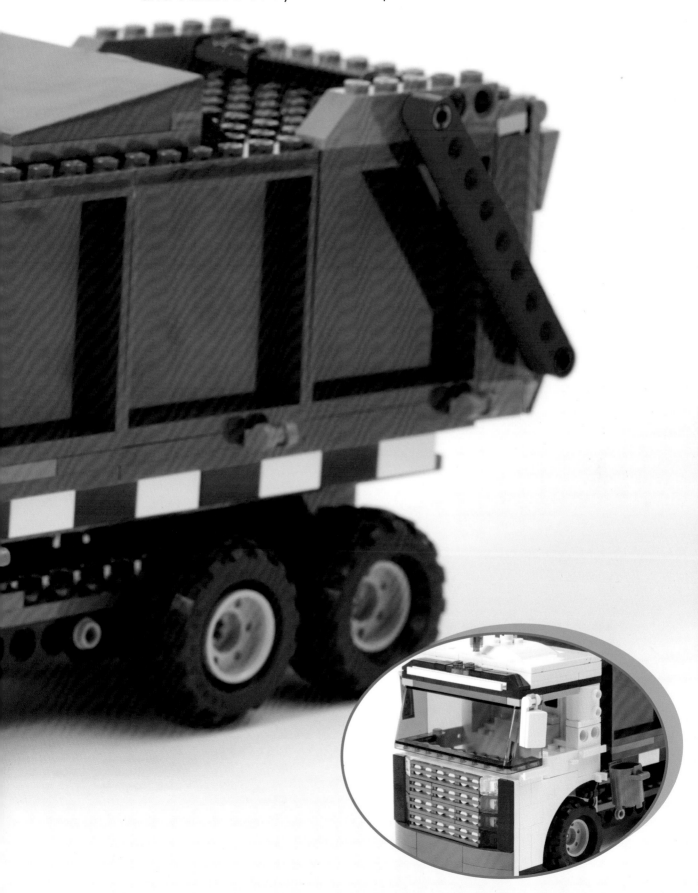

Gardener's Truck

Look at all of the gardening tools! Gardener's trucks carry shovels, mowers, flowers, and other gardening equipment.

Gas Truck

Fill 'er up! This big truck brings gas to gas stations so that people can drive their cars.

Horse Trailer

Sometimes horses need to be moved from one farm or stable to another. Horse trailers bring them where they need to go!

House Mover

Caution: Wide load! This truck can move a whole house from one place to another.

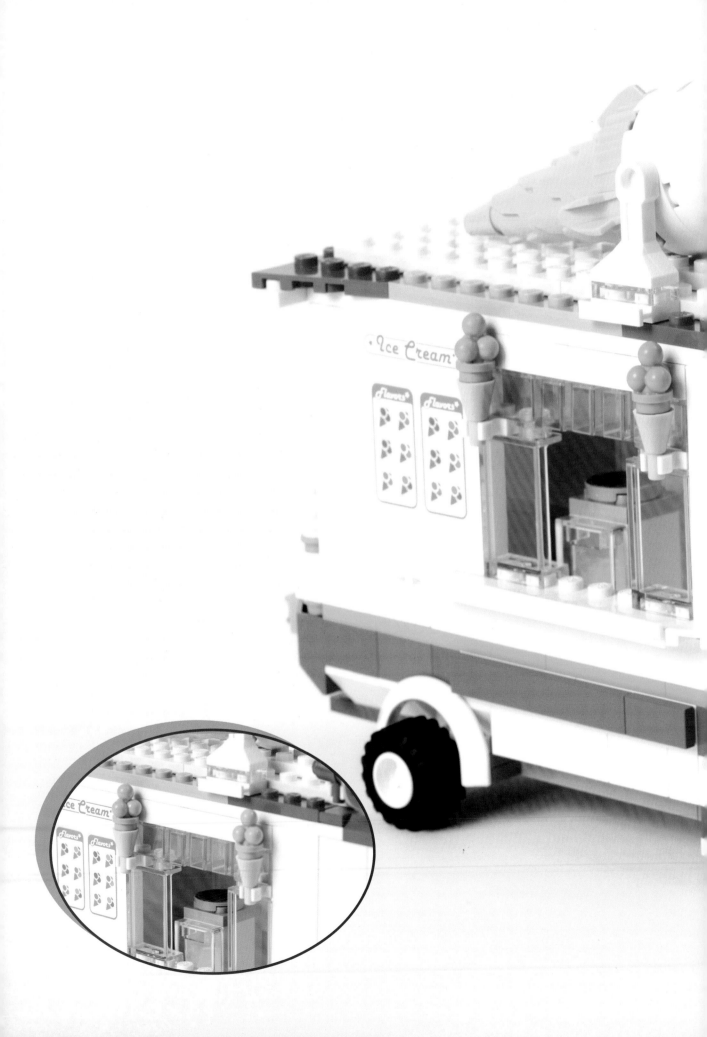

Ice Cream Truck

The most delicious truck there is! Ice cream trucks drive around town selling yummy frozen treats.

Logger

Trees are used to build houses and to make paper. Logging trucks carry the trees from the forest to the sawmill or paper factory.

PN60056

Monster Truck

Monster trucks are for fun! They drive over big things, such as cars or large mounds of dirt, and they have giant wheels.

JC60061

Recycling Truck

Recycling trucks bring used things to centers that make them into new things again. This helps keep the Earth clean!

Tow Truck

If a car gets stuck on the road, a tow truck will help move it! This truck has a big hook to pull cars and other trucks.

PN60056

Tractor Trailer

This big rig moves things all over! It can carry almost anything and drive it to places all over the country.

Sky Pony Press books may be purchased in bulk at special discounts for sales promotion, corporate gifts, fund-raising, or educational purposes. Special editions can also be created to specifications. For details, contact the Special Sales Department, Sky Pony Press, 307 West 36th Street, 11th Floor, New York, NY 10018 or info@skyhorsepublishing.com.

Sky Pony® is a registered trademark of Skyhorse Publishing, Inc.®, a Delaware corporation.

Visit our website at www.skyponypress.com.

10 9 8 7 6 5 4 3 2 1

Manufactured in China, September 2022
This product conforms to CPSIA 2008

Library of Congress Cataloging-in-Publication Data is available on file.

Cover design by Gretchen Schuler-Dandridge
Cover photo credit Amanda Brack

Print ISBN: 978-1-5107-7366-0
Ebook ISBN: 978-1-63220-834-7